To Maddie on her 4th Bday

from

Uncle Jordon + Aunt Kourtnie

A DRAGON'S TALE

"The Dethering"

To order additional copies of this book, contact:
Xlibris Corporation
1-888-795-4274
www.Xlibris.com
Orders@Xlibris.com

4

Once upon a time
In a land not very far away
There were two children lost . . .

gordon
04

...in a dark and scary woodland.

They had been playing hide and go seek with their friends, and so far as their friends knew these two had won the game (which neither could remember ever happening before!)

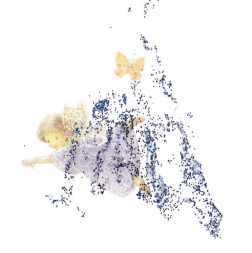

Hiding in the wood was a good idea to begin with, and the Boy still thought so.. "This way!" called the boy, pointing to what looked like a trail back home. "I'm sure.. .this time!"

The little girl was not so sure. Especially since the last time he said as much, he had also said "third time's the charm!"

But she wasn't any more sure where to go than he was.. .they were lost! Truely lost!

Suddenly the trail ended into a small clearing with a still, clear pool of water in the middle. "Wonderful!" shouted the little girl. "I'm so thirsty!"

"HMPF!" grumbled the boy "Girls are so pollyana.. . . ." He stopped what he was about to say with one look from the little girl. She had a way of putting her hands on her hips just like his mom did when she was quite fed up with him.

"I guess I'm a bit thirsty too…." he said, with a smile.

They both knelt by the pool and drank deeply. Suddenly there came a gasp of shock from the edge of the woods. "Oh dears! What have you done?!!" cried a little old man who had wings like a dragonfly.

"What?! Ah, who are YOU? Said the little girl, glancing at the boy, now about to faint!

"Who me?" said the little gnome, wings pointed to his chest "Better the question be "who are YOU!"

"We asked you first!" the girl proclaimed,(yes with her hands placed upon her hips !)

"Well.. ur, that is..yes! That is my name! Pepper Snell, you may call me, Pepper Snell!"

"Pepper Snell!? Pepper smell?!" laughed the little boy regaining his bravado, but stopping when the girl elbowed him in his ribs.

"Ok, Pepper Snell," said the little girl wearily. I'm called Kelly and this is my friend Sean."

"How ya do?" Sean greeted the gnome, reaching down to shake hands with Pepper Snell.

"Very well, thank you, ah.. .no, no!" shouted Pepper Snell, taking back his hand quickly "I'm not doing well! You two have drank from the Dethering!"

"Dethering?" Sean queried "Now look here, you . . . whatever you are, we . . . !" But Kelly had elbowed him again. "Please excuse my friend" soothed Kelly while Sean mumbled to himself. "We meant no harm, we are lost and came upon this water and since we were thirsty. ..what pray tell, sir is a Dethering?"

Pepper Snell muttered to himself a bit, then said brightly."

"We can't cry over crushed blueberries now can we? But once you have drunk from the Dethering you can never go back home!"

"Never go back home!" cried Sean "That's just plain crazy!"

"Hush Sean, I'm sure Mr. Pepper Snell has made some mistake" said Kelly.

"Um, no, little lassie, well there is one way back, but you would not like it." Declared Pepper Snell. "Impossible really.. ..nope, you can never go back" Pepper Snell turned to leave.

"Wait!" cried Sean. "Tell us the way!"

"Yes! Tell us please, Mr. Pepper Snell!? "joined in Kelly.

Pepper Snell paused, rubbed his chin and said "Very well, I will tell you. But once I have told you, it will be as if you promised to do it. Do we have a deal?"

Kelly and Sean looked at each other in wonder, then both smiled and Sean shouted

"We have a deal!"

Pepper Snell also smiled in a wonderful strange manner, and declared.

" Very Well, we have a deal." He then sat them down next to the little pool of water and opened up a hidden sack. "Are you hungry?"

"Yes!" they cried as he pulled out sticky honey cakes, delicious.

"This will give you strength and courage for what you are about to do" Pepper Snell then pulled out a shiny metal object from his pocket.

"This is the key to the endless river" he said, handing it to Kelly. "It is said among my people, that one with enough love, purity and courage will unlock the river and allow the river's waters to flow once more."

"Where shall we go to unlock this.. .river?" asked Kelly.

Pepper Snell pointed to the pool of still water and stated'

"Go through the Dethering to the Otherside"

"Great" mumbled Sean, eyeing the water suspiciously "How are we supposed to breathe?!"

"Ur, ah, well don't worry about that, now off with you!" Suddenly Pepper Snell pushed them into the Dethering!"

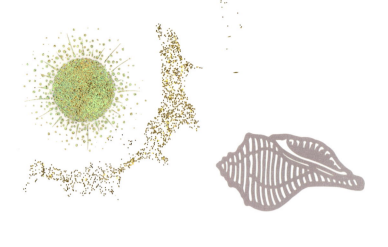

All Sean could remember was a light at the end of ice cold waters. He was sure he had died! Kelly saw a sun at the bottom of a deep well and heard voices singing, but then she hit the sun with a "Splash!" "Wow" thought Sean. "Are we alive?" "Of course we're alive silly" said Kelly, always sure of everything. They were both bobbing up and down in warm salty water by a beautiful beach. They could see a huge mountain touching up to the clouds above.

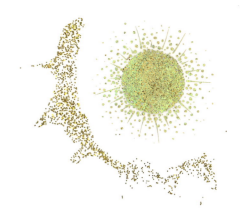

It was a long swim to the shore and by the time they plopped down in the warm sand, they were exhausted. Soon, Kelly and Sean fell asleep to the sound of waves rolling, and seagulls calling, somewhere in their dreams. When they awoke, it was late in the afternoon and they were not alone!

"Hello" said a little girl with wings of lace. She smiled at them and announced "Welcome to the other side. My name is Mint. I suppose the Dethering kicked you out?"

"Dethering! No sir, I mean Ma'am, we were pushed into that stupid puddle!" protested Sean, brushing sand off his pants.

"Pushed?" queried Mint. "Well that's a new one!"

"Mint? Asked Kelly "Do you by chance know of a funny little man named Pepper Snell?"

"Pepper Snell!" whispered Mint" Do you know Pepper Snell?"

"You could say that.." said Sean "He's the one who pushed us into the Dethering!"

"Well!" said Mint" that changes everything!" The Wise ones will want to see you immediately!"" The Wise ones?" asked Kelly "who are they?"

"Oh you will see" said Mint" Come with me!"

Mint pointed the way up a trail, through the forest of pine trees. And they hiked on up the mountain. It wasn't long before the forest opened up into hilly plains that led high, high up the lone peaked summit.

"Kelly! Look!" whispered Sean urgently pointing up into the sky towards the mountain.

"Are those what I think they are!?"

"Dragons!" Kelly gasped, for the first time unsure of a tomorrow.

"Oh, don't be frightened." said Mint "Dragons are quite fun to be around. I should know, my best friend is a dragon!"

"What other creatures live here?" said Kelly gazing into the sky amazed.

"All creatures" said Mint quite matter of fact.

"All of them? " said Sean very surprised!

"Yes" said Mint" Elves and dwarves, fairy folk, gnomes, the tree and water sprites, etc etc and of course dragons!" Suddenly she stopped, looking quite sad.

"Are you not happy here?" asked Kelly.

"Happy?" said Mint "On an island we can never leave, a world that is not ours with a river that never flows?" No, we are not happy here."

They all were silent as Mint stopped atop a hill and they saw before them, a beautiful city! "Wow!" Sean was impressed, while Kelly whispered the words "Beautiful"

"Thank you," said Mint "This may not be our true home, but we stay busy and do our best."

The city was a beehive of activity. Elves and Dwarves, and fairy folk like Mint, bustled about busily finishing up the days work.

Mint led them through the crowds towards a magnificent tower, made of sea shells! Kelly and Sean followed Mint into the tower gate and into a large dome covered courtyard.

There, three of the wisest creatures they had ever surely seen, sat talking amongst themselves quietly.

"They are the wisest among us." whispered Mint. "they spend all their time trying to find the way back home."

Suddenly Mint spoke up in a loud voice, "Hail, Wise Ones!"

The wise ones turned together to look upon them. One was a graceful elven lady, one a peaceful dwarf, the last, behind them, was a large dragon with a beard as long as his tail!"

"Hail, Pepper Mint." Said the Dragon in a deep booming voice that shook the walls. "Who have you brought before us?"

"Two from the outer world, sent by my grand pappy Pepper Snell" cried Mint, bowing and pushing Sean and Kelly to the front of the court.

"Sent?" mumbled Sean, as usual making comments out of order.

"Shhh!" said Kelly looking into the dragon's eyes, "be quiet and let me speak ok?"

The Wise ones waited while Kelly and Sean walked closer. Kelly actually swallowed a lump in her throat, then said.

"Hail Wise ones. I am Kelly O'Rily and this is my friend Sean, Sean McNeal."Kelly then told the wise ones all that had happened to them since becoming lost.

The wise ones looked at each other in silence. The elven lady then spoke.

"Show us this key ,given to you by Pepper Snell, dear child."

Kelly pulled from her pocket the shiny metal object. "Impossible!"

"It cannot be!" "It is the prophesy!"

"But they have drank from the waters of death!" cried the Dwarf silencing them all.

"Waters of Death?" shouted Sean, "Now you just wait one minute, we drank no such thing!"

"The Dethering, young man" said the Dragon in his booming voice sternly "is just that; the death ring!"

"Those who drink of it will surely come to a very bad end!" whispered the dwarf shaking his head sadly.

"What should we do?" asked Kelly.

"Child." said the wise Dragon, "There is nothing you can do."

"No..."said the Elven lady stepping towards Kelly. "There is one thing you can do."

She touched the key Kelly held. "Take this key to the top of the mountain. There you will fmd a door that leads deep into the belly of the abyss. There, if you are true, you will be able to unlock the great river so that it may flow once again, and you will live."

The wise ones turned and said no more. Mint led them out of the tower in silence. Kelly and Sean could both tell that she was terrified . . .

The sun had finally set and the stars were brilliantly lit in the night sky. Mint led them

to a small cottage nestled in a beautiful garden. The little home glowed warm with candlelight.

"You must rest tonight." Said Mint, resolutely opening up the front gate. "This is my grand mammy's place. You shall be our guests!"

"Thank you, Mint" sighed Kelly. " Yeah, thanks . . ." said Sean, his shoulders weighed down with worry.

"It's nothing, really, come meet grand mammy" Mint pushed the door open and sweet smells of herbs and flowers dressed the cozy warm room. A tiny old lady came down the stairs calling "Mint!"

"Mammy! I have so much to tell you! And this is Sean and Kelly; They need a place to stay tonight. .." "Pleasure ,misses Mammy" said Kelly. "Yes" said Sean "Pleasure"

"Indeed. Indeed it is, it is indeed!" said Mammy "Come, I'm sure there will be room for both of you in my loft, in my loft will both of you be!"

"Mammy led them upstairs to a small loft, just big enough for them to stretch out. Kelly and Sean were already asleep before their heads touched the down feather pillows.

Mammy and Mint tucked them in as if they were their own children.

They stepped out of the loft quietly and the children that were lost, now slept soundly all through the night, safe with their dreams of wizards and fairies, dragons and castles, and honey blueberries.

The morning came bright and early, mingled with smells of baking and sweets. Perhaps it was all a dream, Kelly and Sean thought as they stumbled down the stairs(where the Mammy in their dreams became as real as the pile of pancakes steaming in front of them.)

"Good morning to you, you two!" said Mammy cheerily "Did you sleep well, and how well did you sleep?"

"Yes, very well, thank you" said Kelly. Sean was busy eyeing the food like a starving wolf.

"Well, eat up, and up to eat" chanted Mammy "There is plenty, and plenty there is!"
The two children ate hungrily, listening to the morning songbirds at the window, while Mammy busied herself packing something.
"Mammy?" said Kelly, stirring her hot chocolate "Where's Mint?"

— —

"Oh, she's running a few errands, a few errands she will run" rhymed Mammy "She'll be back before long and before long she'll be back"
Sean was still stuffing down the sticky pancakes when a loud crash was heard in the yard.
"Watch the petunias!" someone yelled.
"Sorry" came a deep velvet voice.
Kelly and Sean were both wide eyed with wonder as Mint bounced in the back door smiling from ear to ear!

"I'm back" said Mint to grand mammy

"Are they ready?"

"Yes, dear, oh dear yes!" "Here are your lunches and treats for later, mind you, you mind!"

"Thank you Mammy" chorused all three

"Thank you for everything!"

"Come on, I want you to meet my best friend!" Mint pushed Sean away from his last pancake. "Who is it?" asked Kelly.

"Oh, you'll see" teased Mint pointing them out the door where there in the middle of the petunias sat a large purple dragon trying to straighten a flower!

"I'm sorry, Mint" said the dragon, "I should have watched where I was landing."

"Never mind, Kip" sighed Mint "These are the two children I was telling you about"

The dragon bowed his long shiny purple-scaled neck and smiled a very interesting dragon smile.

"Hello mates, my name is Patrick, but everyone calls me Kip!"

"Hello, Sir Kip." Said Kelly bowing "Wow!" said Sean "this is great, are you for real?"

"Come, come" said Mint "It's time to fly!" Kip helped them all aboard his broad back and with a tremendous leap they were high above the city! It was too incredible for words. Kelly and Sean could now see they were indeed on an island. Kip soared playfully, laughing at Sean and Kelly's faces as they screamed and held on tight to his scales.

"Don't worry," soothed Mint "He's never dropped anyone I know about!"

"Great..." mumbled Sean, quite to himself, as Kelly swallowed hard to keep her breakfast in her tummy.

"There!" announced Mint as they passed over a deep dark crevice in the mountain. A quiet dread enveloped them all as Kip slowly circled down to the meadow beside the abyss.

Kip was shaking his scales nervously as the children and Mint slipped gratefully from his back to the ground.

"This is as far as I can take you" said Kip looking ashamed of himself. "There are some places' even Dragons fear to go."

"Thank you, dear Kip." Said Mint. "You are a true friend."

"Yes, thank you" chorused Sean and Kelly.

"I'll wait right here for you." said Kip leaning up against a tree and pulling out a large book that he took from somewhere to read

"That won't be necessary." said Mint "I'm going with them."

"Inside the abyss!" gasped the Dragon pulling Mint aside "But no one has ever . . ."

"Hush!" whispered Mint "I won't hear of it, now off with you! I mean it!" Kip slipped his book out of sight and stood on his hind legs as if to go.

"No." said Kip, "I'm coming too." Mint grumbled, and Kip hissed, but in the end she knew when a dragon has made up his mind it was useless to argue.

"Then come on, you big lizard, we don't have all day."

Kelly and Sean were well aware something big was amiss, Kip was too big a dragon to whisper without hearing every booming syllable. They wondered if they would survive what was left of this day. A day that started with such bright promise, yet grew gloomier with each passing moment.

Mint led them all to a trail that wound down the dark crevice in the mountain. Smoke billowed out and distant wails of sorrow filled the air.

Soon it grew so dark it could have been evening, and it became deathly quiet, not even the wind came to rustle the leaves upon the ground.

"This can't be good!" whispered Kip (loudly) looking all about the silent forest deep in the abyss.

"Be quiet Kip!" said Mint." You are scaring the children!"

"Scaring the children!" cried Kip "My scales are about ready to jump off!"

"Look!" said Sean pointing up the trail "Is that the door we are looking for?"

"The doorway to the Abyss!" Mint said in awe.

"Doesn't seem so bad . . ." said Kelly.

"Doesn't seem too scary" said Sean looking round about.

"Doesn't seem too bad and scary?" said Kip looking back behind him. "Are you nuts? This place is evil! Evil! Evil! Evil! How did I ever get talked into this?"

The four of them stood before the door in silence, thinking. Mint patted Kip's head comfortingly. Sean shifted from one foot to another and Kelly traced the intricate words on the door with her finger. Suddenly Kelly pushed hard on the door. "No Kelly! Don't . . ." said Mint, but it was too late. Everyone fell silent again as the huge door parted inwards. "Creeeeeek". Warm, moist air rushed out of the darkness as If the mountain had been holding it's breath for ages.

"I was hoping it would have been harder to open" said Sean

"Me too" said Kip

"We're going to need some light." Said Mint rummaging through her pack.

"Yes, here we go.." She pulled out a number of clear candles and handed one to each of them.

As they lit their candles and went into the darkness, their little sticks began to glow brightly.

"Stay alert, everyone." Said Mint "We don't know what lives here"

Cautiously they made their way into the depths of the mountain tunnels. Time seemed to stand still, but it also seemed as if they had walked forever.

Suddenly the tunnel walls opened wide into a huge cavern.

"I'm hungry" announced Sean

"Me too" said Kip. "Well," said Mint. "I guess we can stop here for a bit and eat, I don't see or hear anything scary. . . . right now . . ."

Kelly said nothing and wandered over to a gigantic pillar of stone. Sitting down she toyed with something in her pockets. .~.

They ate quietly, except for Sean and Kips "mmmms" of joy eating Mammy's delicious sweet rolls. Kelly ate nothing and Mint grew concerned.

Then Kelly jumped up and stared into the darkness. "What's wrong, Kelly?" said Mint.

"Shhh! I hear something coming!"

The sound was faint, but you could feel

the sound more than hear it, more like a small earthquake I'd say.

The sound grew and the floor trembled and then it stopped just as suddenly as it had begun!

"Wha..what do you think that was . . . ?" Sean grabbed Kelly-more to protect himself than her. "Be quiet!" whispered Kelly, still staring out into the fathomless darkness.

Suddenly a voice hissed just beyond their candlelight.

"Who dares to enter my Abysssss!"

No one answered. No one dared.

Again the voice came, but much louder this time.

"Who dares to enter my Abyss!!!"
Kelly stepped towards the sound. "It is I!
Keeper of the key to the Endless River!"
The others watched in horror, unable to move!
"Come forward, Keeper!" said the voice. Kelly
stepped farther into the darkness, until her
candle illuminated a most monstrous sight!
A huge lumpy, black and miserable dragon, with
large sleepy eyes that were dull with sorrow. .
"Keeper, you have come too late" The great
ugly dragon said. "There is no river, and
nothing you can do here. The dethering
is too strong.. ..too set in it's ways. There
is no hope to free the river and heal these
wounds:—The great lumpy dragon covered
with sores turned to leave. But then Kip
bravely came forward.

"Great Lady, how came you to this dark and sad place?" Kip smiled at her, a cute dragon toothy smile-sort of.

He continued" Come back with us, come out in the sunshine, you don't need to stay here!"

"No lad" The sad lumpy Dragon lady said "My place is here. It is my tomb, my well deserved punishment."

"Please, great lady." begged Kip politely seeing past her scary appearance." I know of no crime worthy of such a punishment as this!"

"As well you never do." Said the dragon as she turned to go once more" As well you never do. Be gone with you now! There is nothing you can do here!"

"No!" Kelly shouted. "No. I will not go! You know it isn't too late. You've just given up! You've given in and forgotten what it was in the light! You.. you.. .you sad old dragon!"

The old dragon's eyes suddenly blazed and

52

she rose to her full height!

"HOW DARE YOU!" she snorted, breathing fire from her mouth. "Who are YOU to know anything? You have NO idea!"

"Yes I do!" cried Kelly

"Things happen for a reason! A greater reason.. ..there is always hope.. .always time to change." Kelly raised the key high above her head and commanded, "show me the Endless River!"

The great dragon actually bowed her head, and said, "As you wish." She then moved aside and there before Kelly was a dark and loathsome pool. Kelly gasped as the others gathered around her, their new leader! An overwhelming sadness came upon them, and Mint began to weep softly.

"How could this happen to the everlasting

waters?" Mint cried, wiping her tears on her sleeve.

"Once, long ago," said the great sad dragon," the worlds were one, and the great river flowed giving life to all creatures. We all lived together in peace until one day . . . that horrible day I separated the world.

"You did this?" Kip said shocked.

"Yes," the great dragon said with a far away look in her dull eyes. " But I was mistaken! I thought I was right to separate us from man. Mankind was dangerous, and careless with the land and living things. I could see the greed in their eyes! She looked fiercely at Sean.

"Me? I'm just a kid!" protested Sean.

"Yes.. .just a harmless little child." She said smiling sadly, "How was I suppose to know that separating us would make that danger come alive! For without us in your world, man fought wars for money, land and power! Millions died for the greed of a few wicked men we dragons would have easily gobbled up in a second!"

"But you didn't know!" cried Kelly "You were just being protective!"

-~~>

The great dragon sighed a very deep sigh, and suddenly touched a great tear from her eyes. Surprised, the great dragon began to cry great wrenching sobs, that echoed in the cavern.

The tears gathered quickly into a small pool that ran into the loathsome pool.

Suddenly, light shone around the edges of the pool. The more the tears spilled, the more light began to shine.

"What's happening?" asked Sean. "The spell must be broken!" whispered Mint.

"Look!" Kip cried pointing into the now brilliantly lit pool of water. A small figure came out of the pool, a familiar form...."Grandpappy!" cried Mint, running to embrace Pepper Snell. "Don't push me in!" said Sean. (everyone ignored him . . .)

"Oh child!" cried Pepper Snell" I though I would never lay eyes on my lassie again!"

"Pepper Snell, did you know this would happen?" asked Kelly. "No child," said Pepper Snell holding Mint tightly, "No I did not, but I hoped it would." He released Mint and strode with his short little legs over to the quietly sniffing Dragon.

"Open your eyes, great lady." He said touching her hands that covered her eyes. "Look what your tears have done!"

The great Dragon removed her hands with one final great sniffle. Then stared in awe at her reflection in the now beautiful pool. She was young again! And smooth and beautiful! (by dragon standards) "How . . . ?"

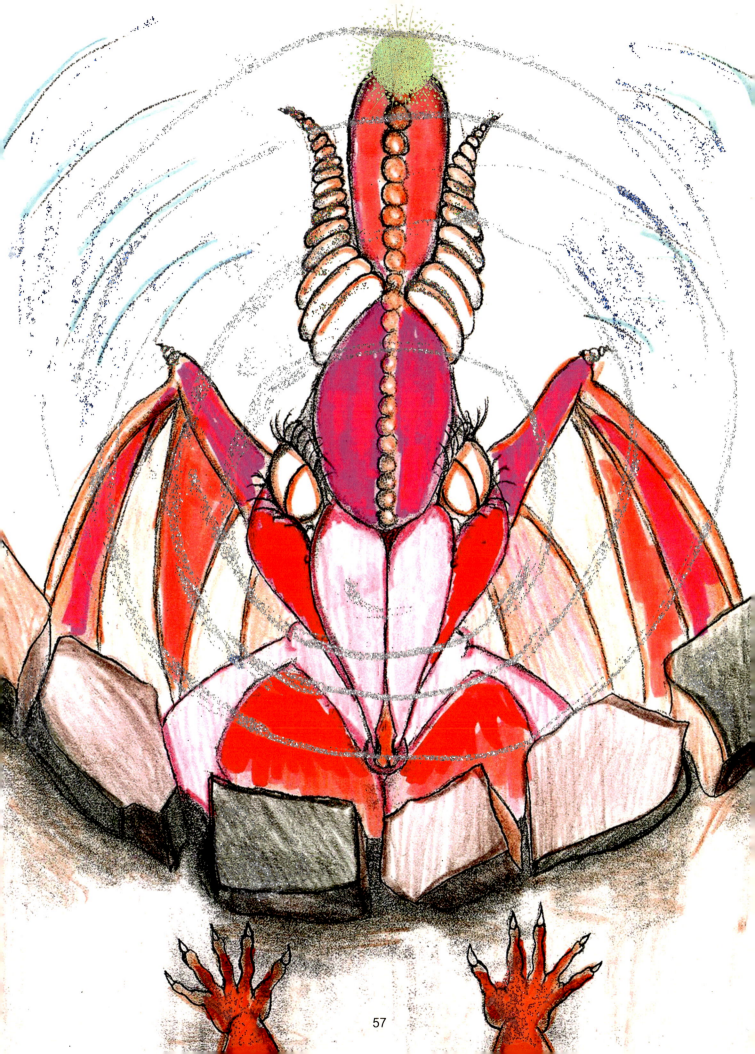

She couldn't find any words.

"Sometimes," quoted Pepper Snell "It takes the deepest sorrows to find the greatest joys."

"Is it done, then? Does the great river also flow once more?" she asked.

"No, great lady." He said "but the worlds are once *more* connected if not one. We are free once *more* to travel the whole of our mother land!"

"But how?" asked the great lady dragon, still looking in the shiny pool at her reflection.

"I do not know." Said Pepper Snell "Sometimes, tears are heard by the powers on high and are the most potent of magic miracles."

"And what about my magic key?" asked Kelly handing him the shiny metal object he had given her. "Oh that!" he laughed, "Just something I found in the woods one day." Kelly eyed it disbelieving him, and then smiled too. "If it makes no difference to you, I'd like to keep it."

"Indeed!" said Pepper Snell, "Good job! All of you! Superbly well done!"

Sean and Kip stood up straight with pride.

"Today will be a day of celebration, and for many If not all years to come!

Come! Let us go tell the Wise ones!"

And that is just what they did, and all the creatures rejoiced at the news of returning to their home. And it was not many years *before* the whole world was at peace once again, along with some very well fed dragons, when the wicked ones came their way.

Even though the great river ceased to flow, a new river was born in the hearts of all the creatures of Earth. People found themselves wondering how they ever had lived otherwise.

The years went by, the children grew.. .but that is another dragon's tale . . . .

THE END...

Story By
Gordon Sean McWhorter
Dedicated to his daughter
Kelen May